For Ame, who helped me out of my cave
—*A. L.*

For Ted R., for always asking about this one
—*S. M.*

SIMON & SCHUSTER BOOKS FOR YOUNG READERS • An imprint of Simon & Schuster Children's Publishing Division • 1230 Avenue of the Americas, New York, New York 10020 • Text copyright © 2016 by Adam Lehrhaupt • Illustrations copyright © 2016 by Scott Magoon • All rights reserved, including the right of reproduction in whole or in part in any form. • SIMON & SCHUSTER BOOKS FOR YOUNG READERS is a trademark of Simon & Schuster, Inc. • For information about special discounts for bulk purchases, please contact Simon & Schuster Special Sales at 1-866-506-1949 or business@simonandschuster.com. • The Simon & Schuster Speakers Bureau can bring authors to your live event. For more information or to book an event, contact the Simon & Schuster Speakers Bureau at 1-866-248-3049 or visit our website at www.simonspeakers.com. Book design by Chloë Foglia • The text for this book was set in Bodoni and hand lettered. • The illustrations for this book were rendered digitally. Manufactured in China • 0616 SCP • First Edition
10 9 8 7 6 5 4 3 2 1
Library of Congress Cataloging-in-Publication Data
Names: Lehrhaupt, Adam. | Magoon, Scott, illustrator.
Title: I will not eat you / Adam Lehrhaupt ; illustrated by Scott Magoon.
Description: First edition. | New York : Simon & Schuster Books for Young Readers, [2016] | Summary: A dragon resists the urge to eat the animals that approach his cave.
Identifiers: LCCN 2015029655| ISBN 9781481429337 (hardcover) | ISBN 9781481429344 (eBook)
Subjects: | CYAC: Dragons—Fiction. | Animals—Fiction. | Friendship—Fiction.
Classification: LCC PZ7.L532745 Iap 2017 | DDC [E]—dc23 LC record available at http://lccn.loc.gov/2015029655

I Will Not EAT YOU

Adam Lehrhaupt & Scott Magoon

A Paula Wiseman Book

Simon & Schuster Books for Young Readers

New York London Toronto Sydney New Delhi

Theodore lived in a cave.

It was a quiet cave,
and that's the way he liked it.

One morning, a bird flew up to the cave.
It tweeted and squawked at Theodore.

tweet tweet
Squawk Squawk

Theodore thought,
Does it want me to eat it?

tweet

But Theodore wasn't hungry.

"Go away, silly bird,"
he whispered.
"I will not eat you."

The bird flew away.

Later, a wolf jogged up to the cave.
It howled at Theodore.

Theodore thought,
Perhaps I should eat it?

But Theodore wasn't hungry.

"Go away, loud wolf," he grunted.
"I will not eat you."

The wolf jogged away.

That afternoon, a tiger ran up to the cave.
It growled at Theodore.

GRRRR

Theodore thought,
Should I eat it?

But Theodore still wasn't hungry.

"Go away, rumbly tiger," he huffed.
"I will not eat you."

The tiger ran away.

That evening, a boy galloped up to the cave.
The boy roared at Theodore.

RAAAAAAAAAAAA

Seriously? thought Theodore.
I should eat it.

Theodore *was* getting hungry.

"**Don't bother me,
pesky boy,**"

he bellowed,

"**or I will eat you.**"

The boy did not go away.

He roared again.
This upset Theodore.

RARRAR
RARR
RA
RA
A
R
R
RAAAARR!
A
A

The boy poked.

"That's IT!" Theodore snarled.

Theodore chased the boy.

"I WILL eat you!"

Until . . .

The boy
fell
down.

Before Theodore could gobble him up, something unexpected happened.

The boy
laughed.

Ha, ha, ha, ha!

HA,HA,HA,HA!

That made Theodore laugh.

And it's hard to eat someone
when you're sharing a laugh.

Theodore still lived in a cave.

But now the cave was extra quiet.

Because Theodore
was outside playing.

I can always eat him later,
thought Theodore.